This book belongs to

_____

Young Readers Book Club presents…

Olive and the Magic Hat

Eileen Christelow

Clarion Books / Ticknor & Fields / New York

Clarion Books
Ticknor & Fields, a Houghton Mifflin Company
Text and illustrations: © 1987 by Eileen Christelow

Library of Congress Cataloging-in-Publication Data

Christelow, Eileen.
Olive and the magic hat.

Summary: Playing with their father's hat, Olive
and Otis Opossum accidentally drop it on Mr. Foxley
who becomes convinced that the hat is magical.
[1. Opossums—Fiction.   2. Foxes—Fiction.
3. Brothers and sisters—Fiction]   I. Title.
PZ7.C452301   1987   [E]   87-672
ISBN 0-89919-513-X

C D   1 2 3

"Tonight is Father's birthday party," said Olive. "Are we going to give him a present?"

"It's on the dining room table," said Mother. "When we finish making the cake, we'll wrap it."

On the table, Olive found a tall black hat.

"I think it's a magic hat," said Olive.

"Me too," said her brother Otis.

"It's a fancy dress hat and not to be touched with sticky paws," said their mother. She put the chocolate birthday cake into the oven.

"I still think it's a magic hat," said Olive.

  While Mother went up to the attic to search for
wrapping paper, Olive shared cake batter lickings
with Otis. They looked at the tall black hat.
  "If I say some magic words, something might
happen," said Olive.
  "Say some magic words," said Otis.

Olive stood on a stool, closed her eyes, and said some magic words. She waved her paws and swayed back and forth.

"Watch out!" squealed Otis.

Olive teetered and tottered...

…and toppled on top of Otis.

Otis bumped into the table and knocked the tall black hat…

...right out of the open window.

When Olive picked herself up, she couldn't find the hat anywhere.

"I think I said the wrong magic words," she groaned. "I made the hat disappear!"

"I think I knocked it out of the window," said Otis.

Olive and Otis looked out of the window.

"Oh no!" whispered Olive. "There's Mr. Foxley!"

"He has the hat!" said Otis.

Mr. Foxley was talking to himself. "I don't believe it!" he muttered. "This hat fell out of the sky, right onto my head! It must be my lucky day!"

Mr. Foxley walked down the path toward the river, wearing the hat and a smile.

"We have to get it back!" cried Olive. "Father will be home soon and it's almost time for his party. Mother will be so angry!"

"You can't get it back," said Otis.

"Mr. Foxley is a fox. He might eat you!"

But Olive raced out of the house and down the path.
Otis followed.

They found Mr. Foxley settling himself by the river to
do some fishing. He laid the hat in the grass and
closed his eyes.

"This is my chance," whispered Olive.

Olive found a long, hooked branch. She used it to
slowly pull the hat toward her.

Mr. Foxley twitched his nose and opened one eye.

"STOP!" Mr. Foxley yelled.
He lunged for the hat—just missing
Olive's nose. Olive held her breath.
She didn't dare move.

But Mr. Foxley was too excited about the hat to notice Olive.

"Amazing!" he gasped. "A walking hat! Maybe it's magic. I must show it to Mrs. Foxley." He hurried down the path toward home.

"You sure fooled him," said Otis.

"But he still has the hat!" wailed Olive. "How are we going to get it back?"

"Mr. Foxley left his fishing pole behind," said Otis.

Several minutes later, Mr. Foxley was almost home. But, just as he came strolling under the ledge that overlooked his path...

...the hat suddenly jumped off his head.

"Oh no you don't!" shouted Mr. Foxley. He leaped into the air and grabbed the hat just in time. But he had to pull and tug to get it back.

"That's some powerful magic!" he gasped.

"There is only one thing to do with a walking, jumping, powerful magic hat," said Mr. Foxley. He pulled a piece of string out of his pocket and tied the hat to his head.

"Now we'll never get it back," said Otis.

"We have to," said Olive.

Mr. Foxley walked on to his den.

Olive and Otis hid near Mr. Foxley's window and listened as he told his wife about his walking, jumping, powerful magic hat.

"I don't like it!" they heard Mrs. Foxley say.
"Next thing you know, it will be talking."

"Nonsense," said Mr. Foxley.

A few moments later when Mr. Foxley was reading
the comics, he heard a voice.

"P-s-s-s-s-t!"

"Did you say something, my dear?" Mr. Foxley asked
his wife.

"I did not," she said. "But someone did."

They looked out of the window, but all they saw was
a bush.

So they sat down to read again.

"P-s-s-s-s-t!" said the voice. "This is your hat talking!"

"I knew it!" shrieked Mrs. Foxley.

She untied the hat and threw it out of the window.

"Don't!" shouted Mr. Foxley. But when he saw the bush catch the hat and run down the path, he grew light-headed and trembly-kneed. He had to lie down for the rest of the day.

Olive and Otis ran all the way home.

"Where have you been?" scolded Mother. "I was so worried! And what happened to the hat?"

"I tried to do a magic trick," said Olive.

"It didn't work very well," said Otis.

Mother was very cross. She told Olive and Otis to clean the hat and wrap it at once.

"Your father is sitting in the garden and it's time for his party."

Olive and Otis brushed off the hat and tried to wrap it. But the package looked terrible.

"I have a better idea," said Olive.

When Mother brought out the birthday cake, Olive
sang "Happy Birthday."

"Where is the present?" whispered Mother.

"It is about to appear," said Olive.

She waved her paws and said some magic words, and suddenly…

...the hat dropped onto her father's head.

"I don't believe it!" gasped her father. "This fancy dress hat just fell out of the sky right onto my head. How did that happen?"

"I can't imagine…" said Mother.

Olive winked at Otis. "It must be a magic hat," she said.